EASTER
Dot-to-Dot

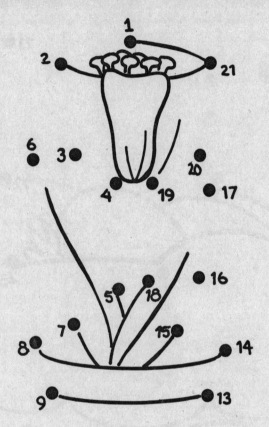

All trademarks are the property of
Western Publishing Company, Inc.

A GOLDEN BOOK®
Western Publishing Company, Inc.
Racine, Wisconsin 53404

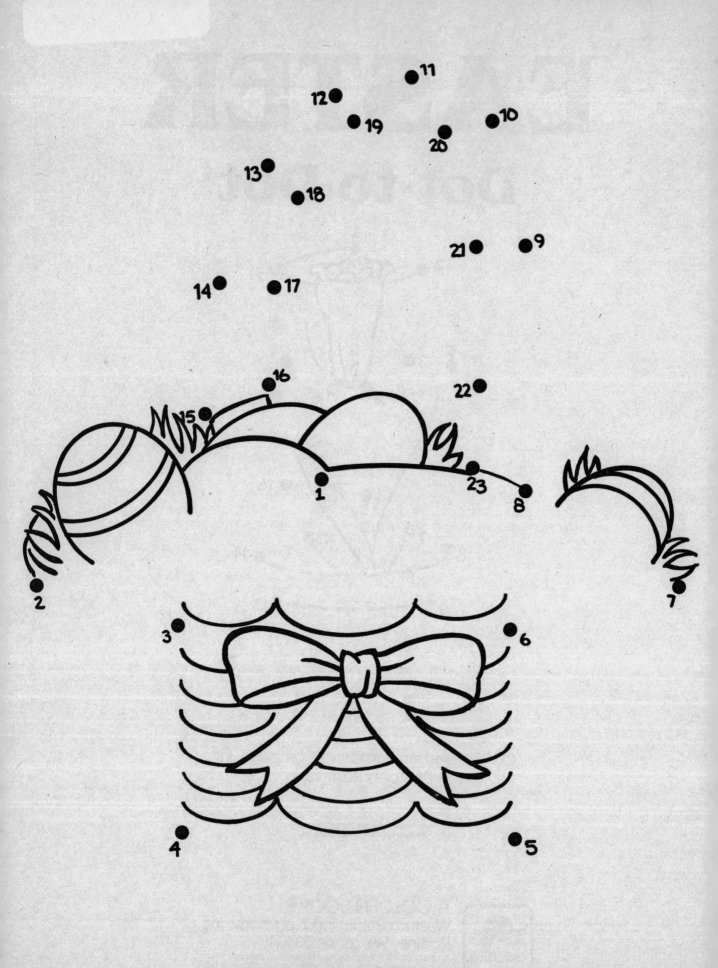

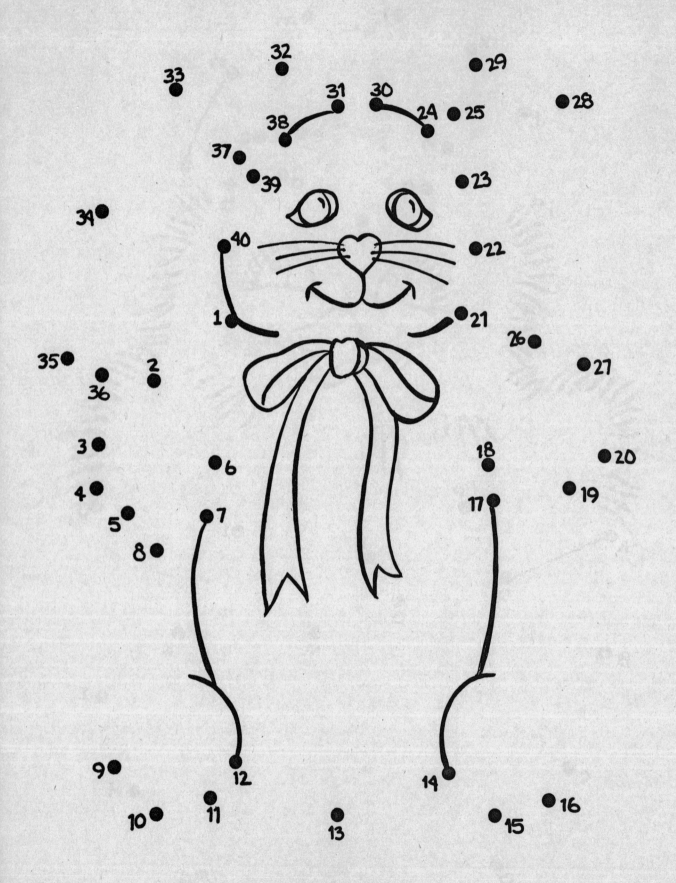

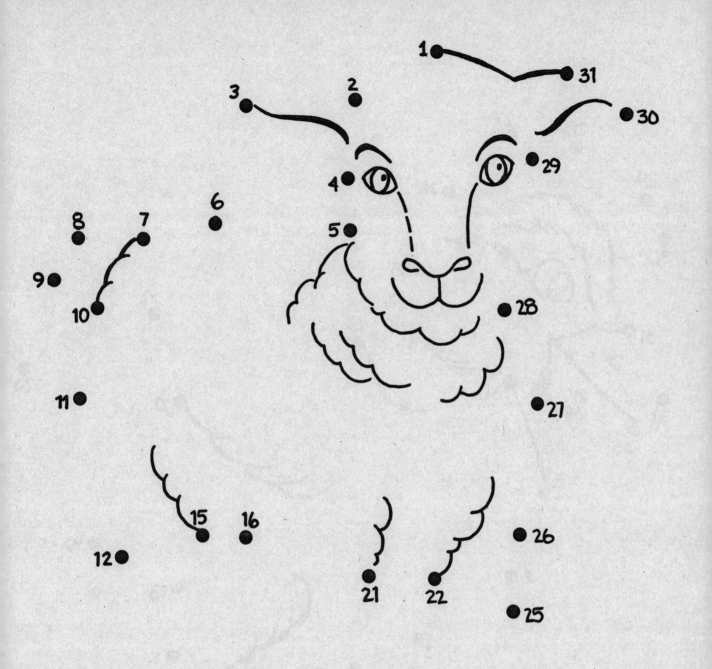

1

31

3

2

30

29

4

6

5

8

7

9

28

10

11

27

15

16

26

12

21

22

25

17

18

19

20

13

14

23

24

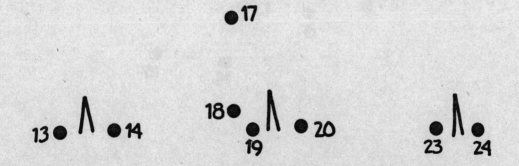

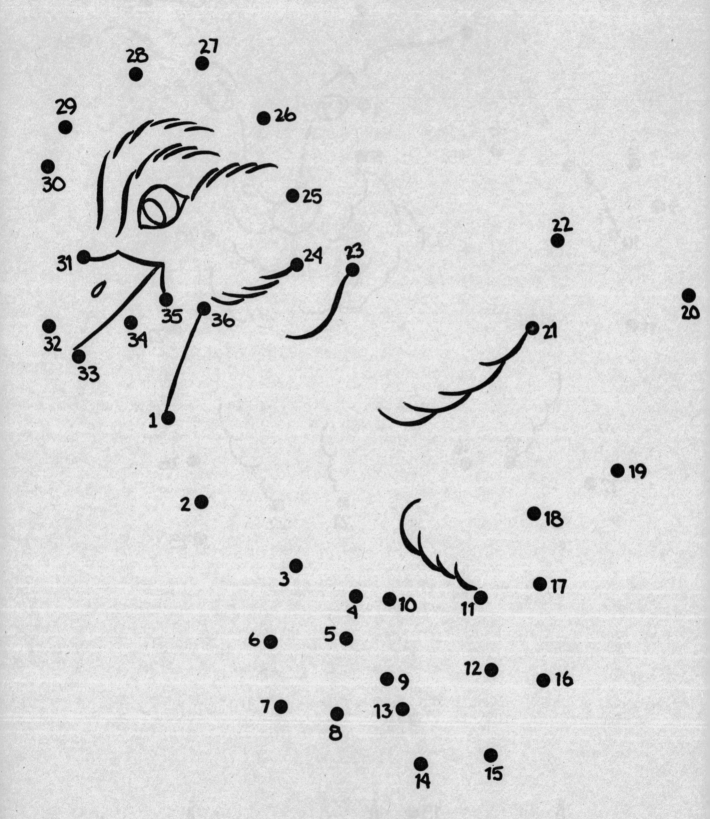

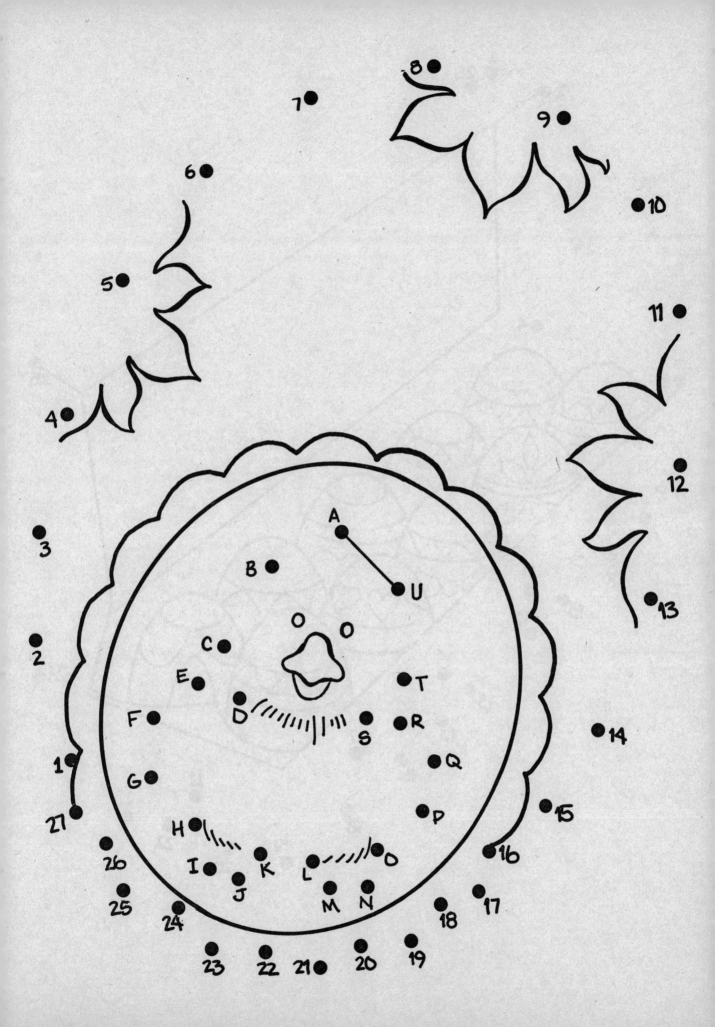

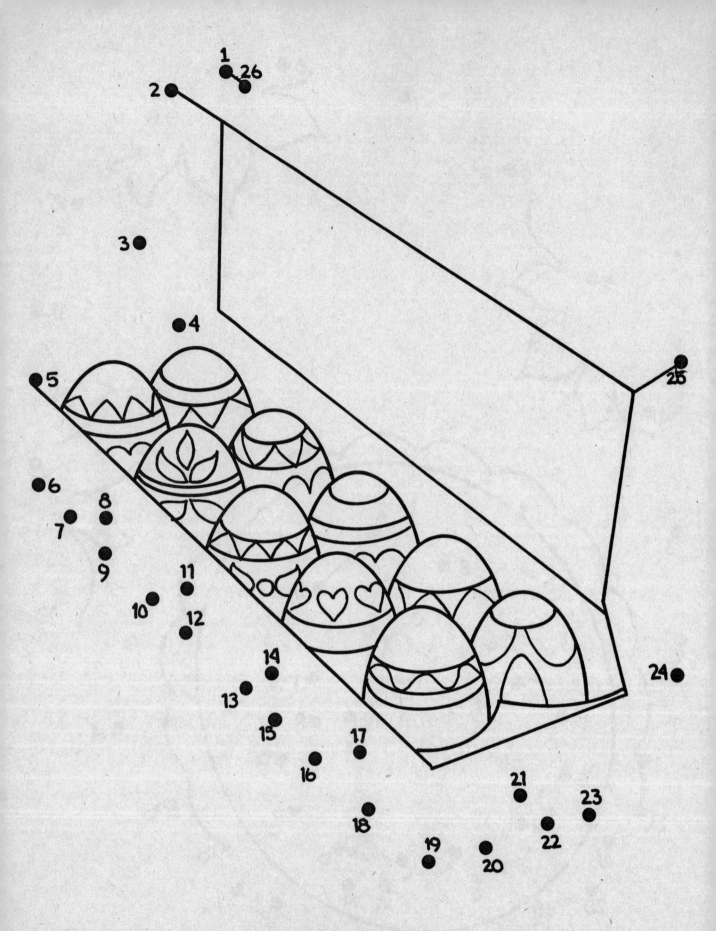

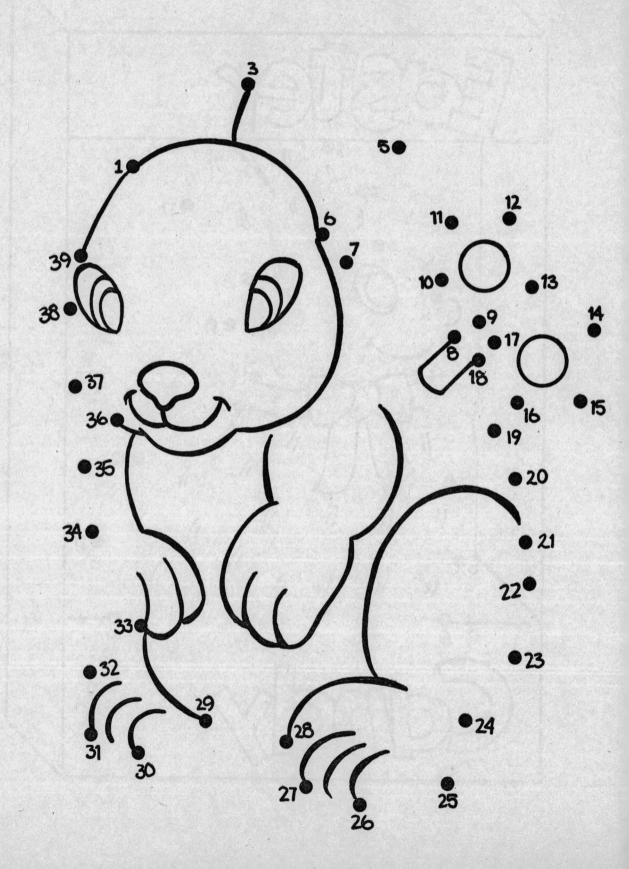

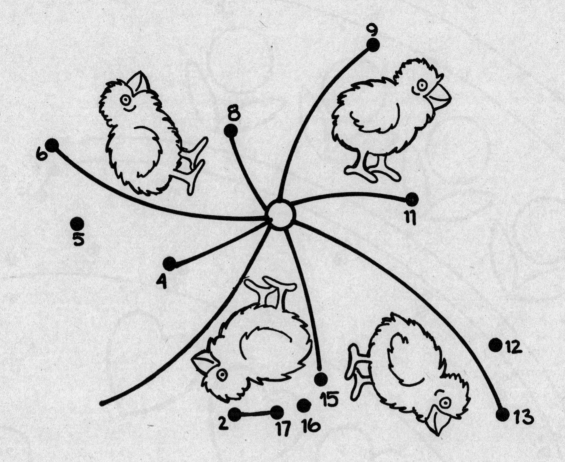

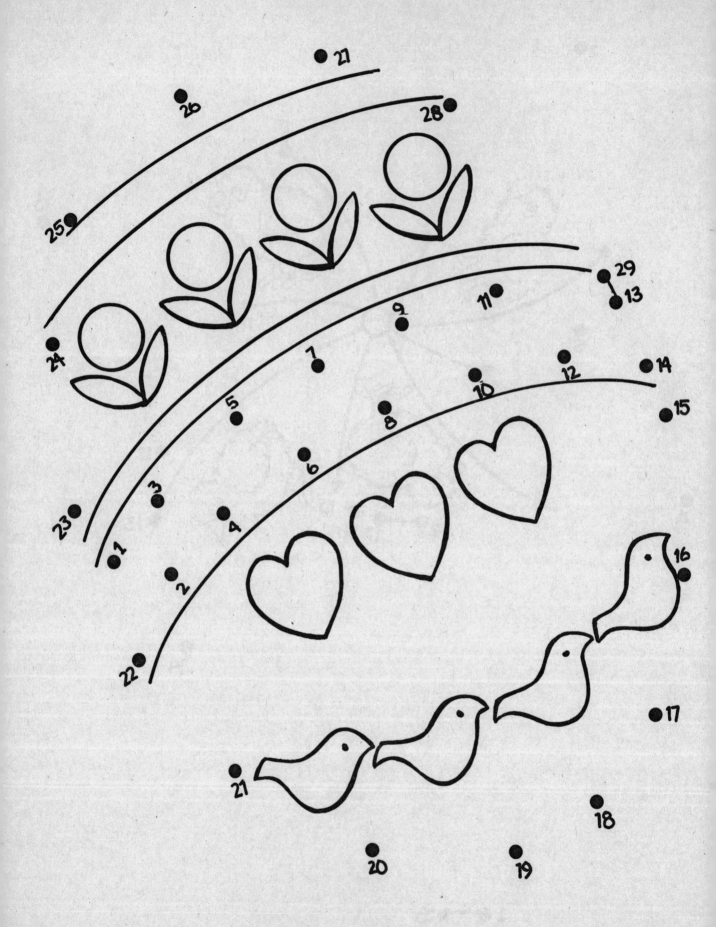

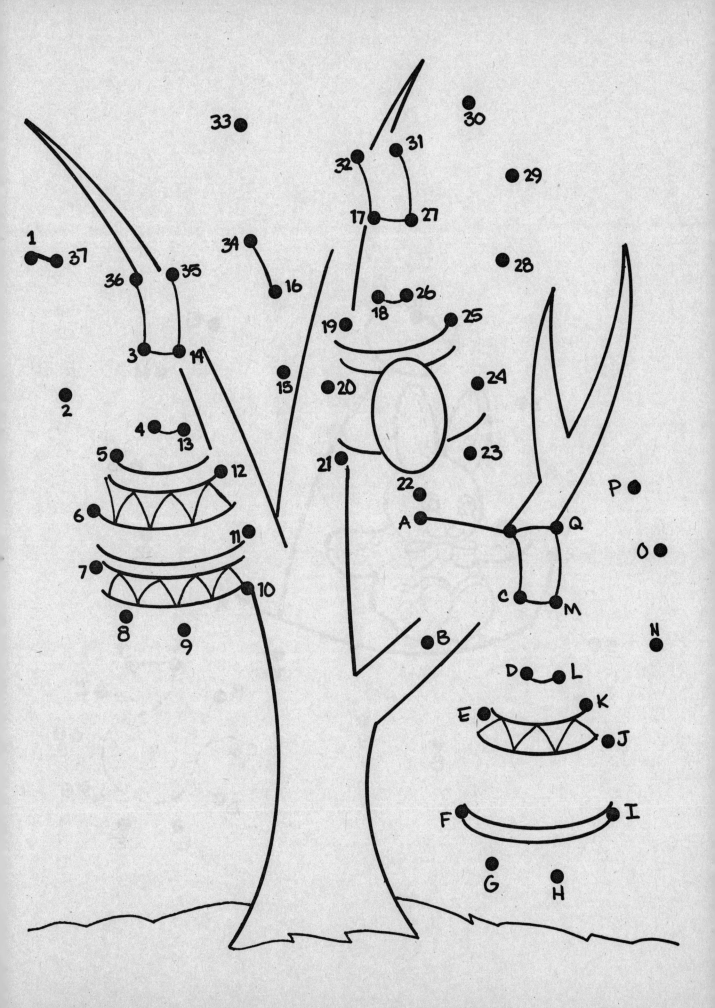

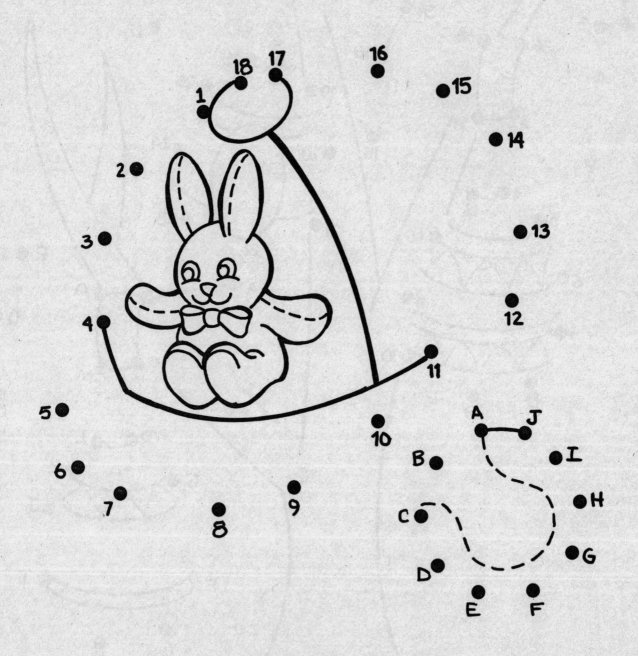

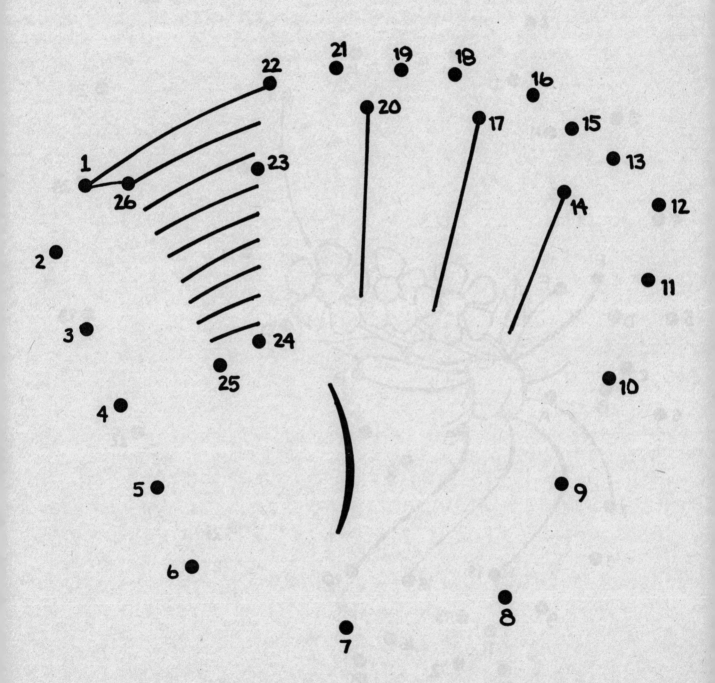

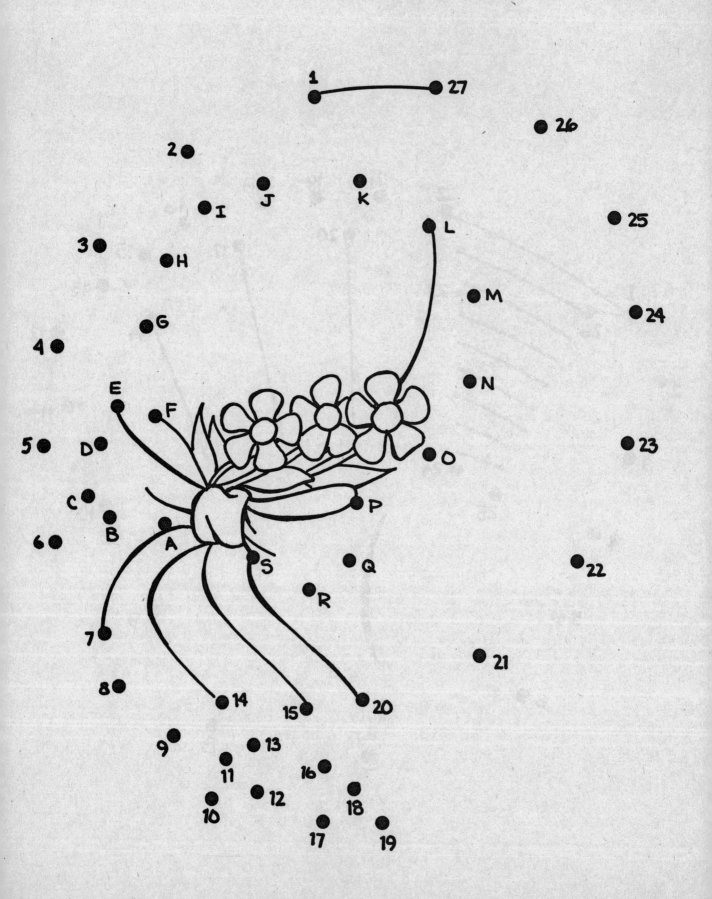

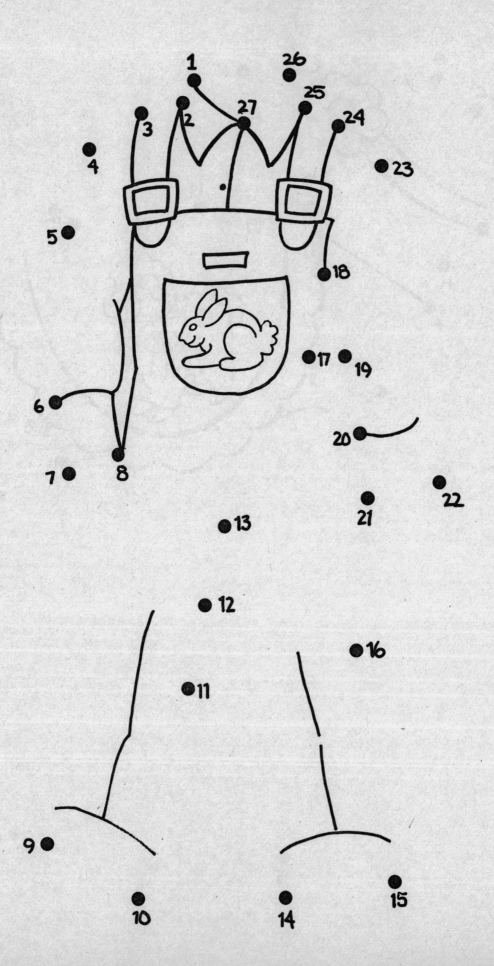

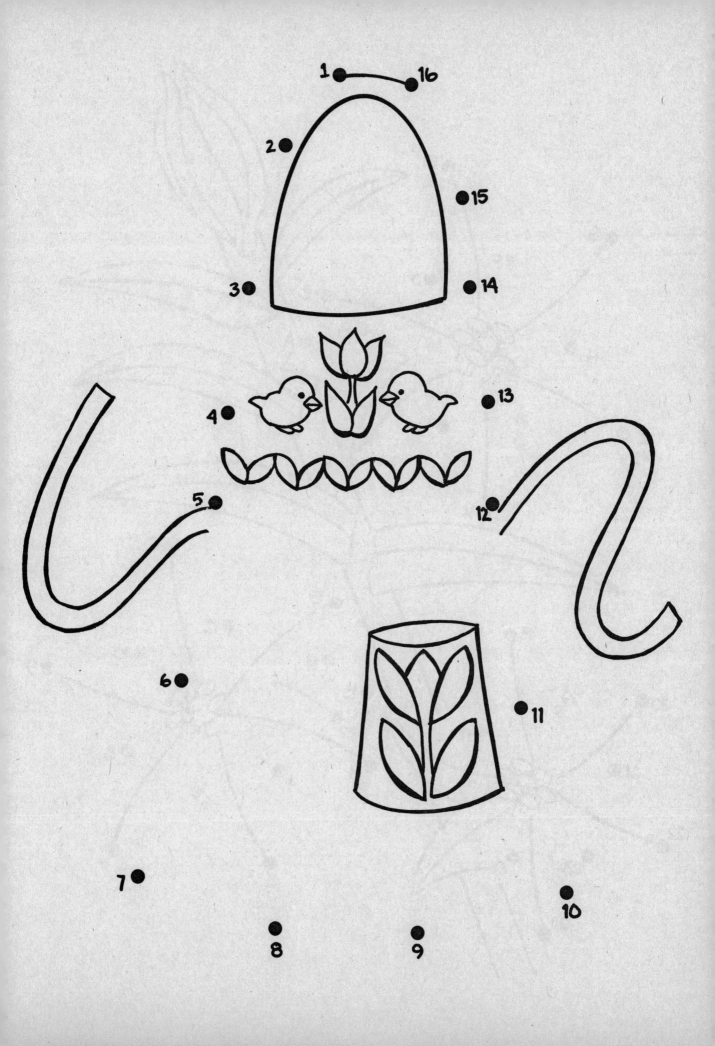

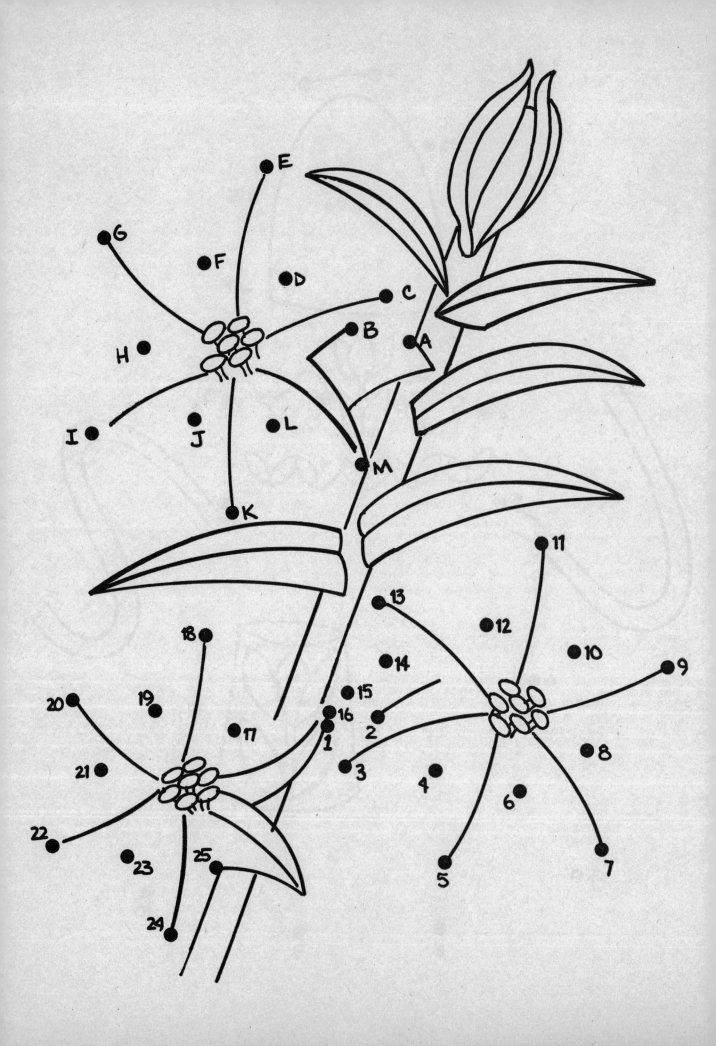

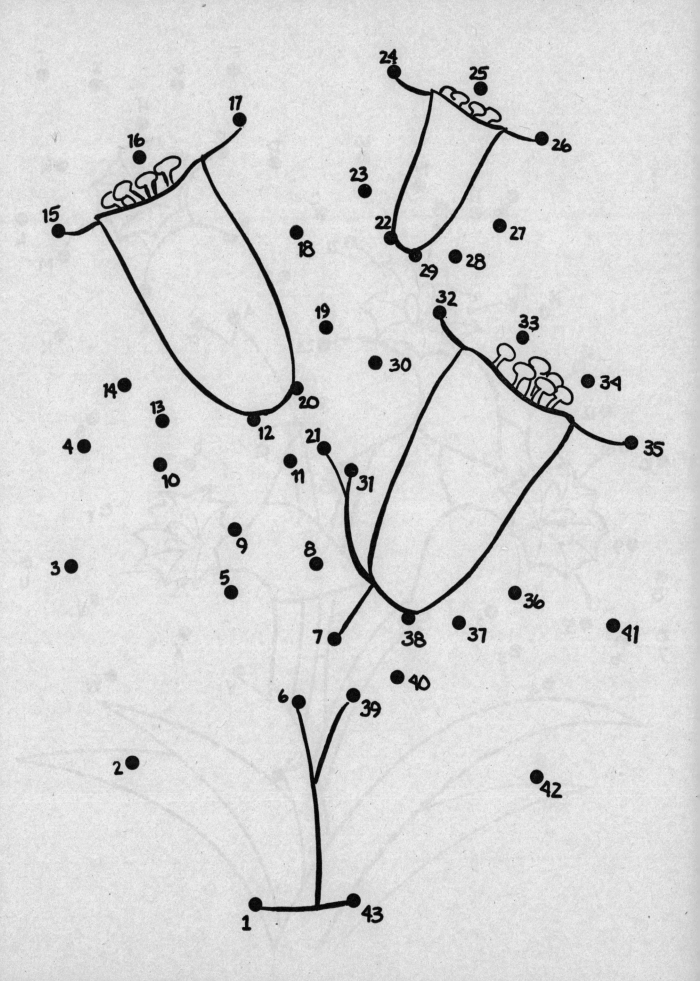

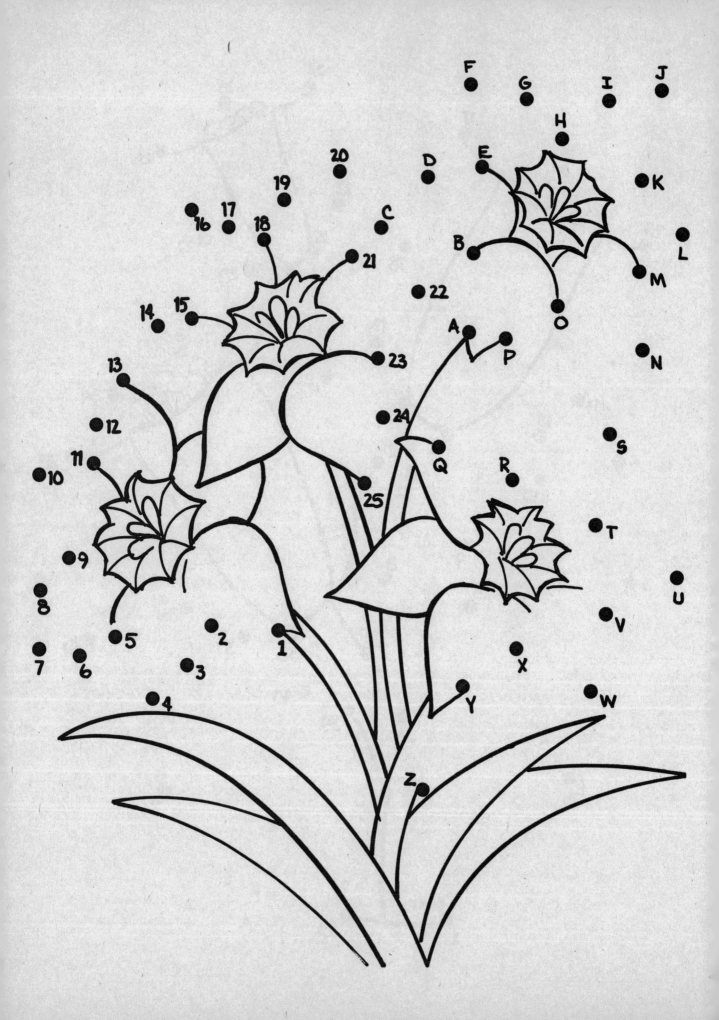

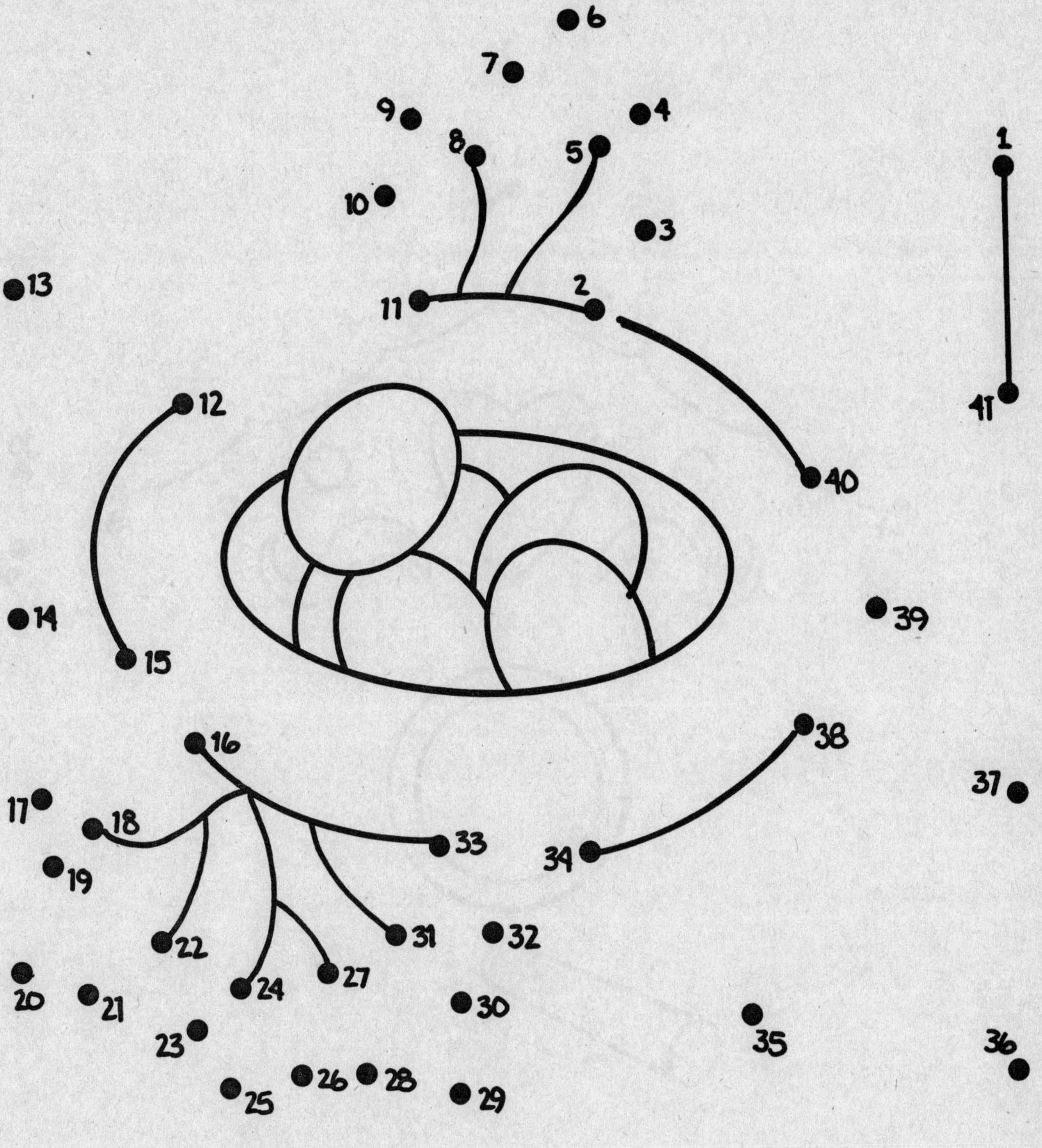
1
2
3
4
5
6
7
8
9
10
11
12
13
14
15
16
17
18
19
20
21
22
23
24
25
26
27
28
29
30
31
32
33
34
35
36
37
38
39
40
41

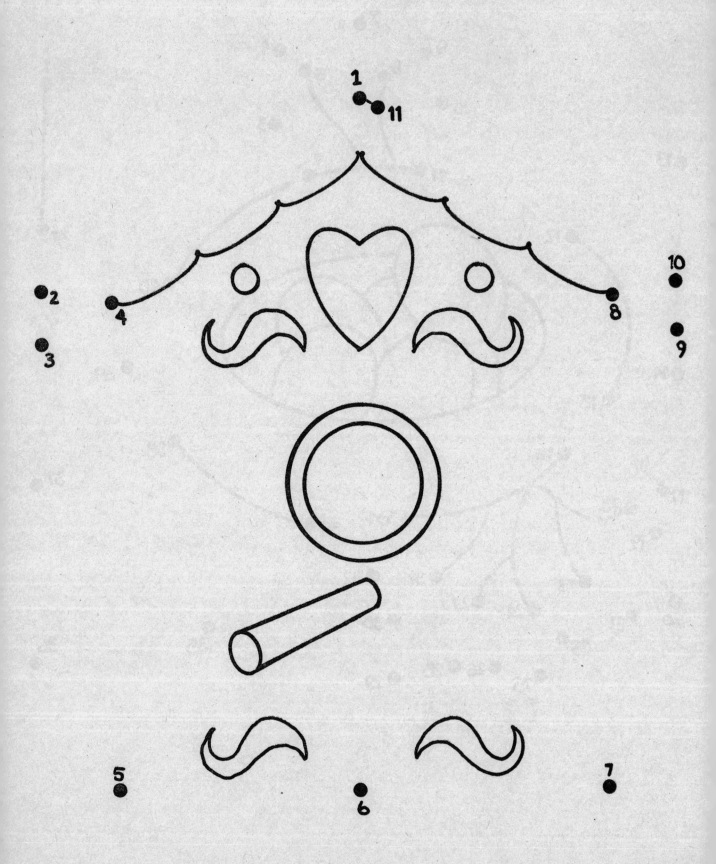

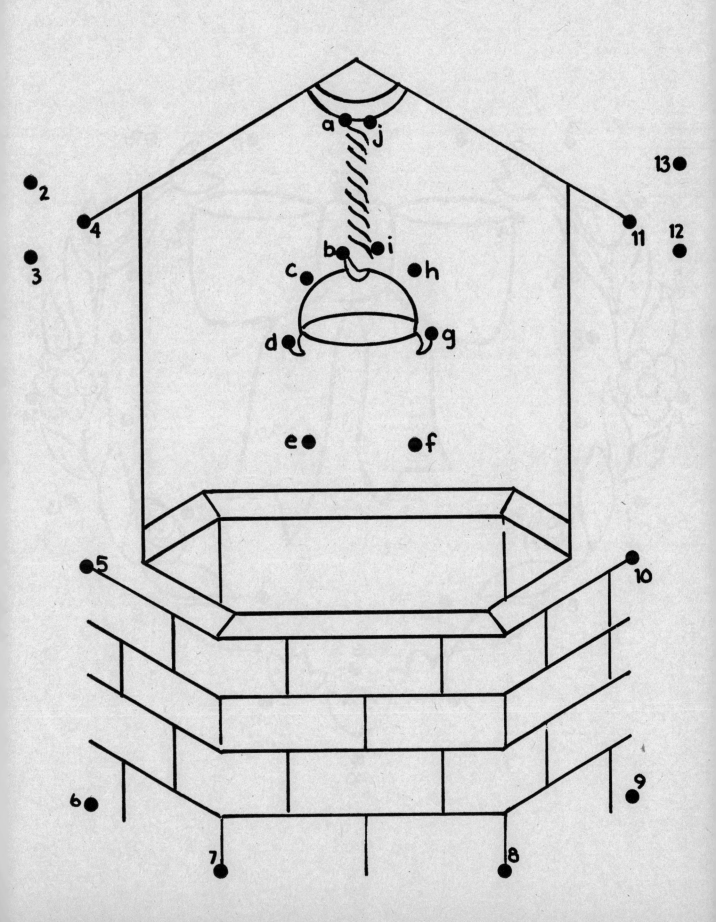

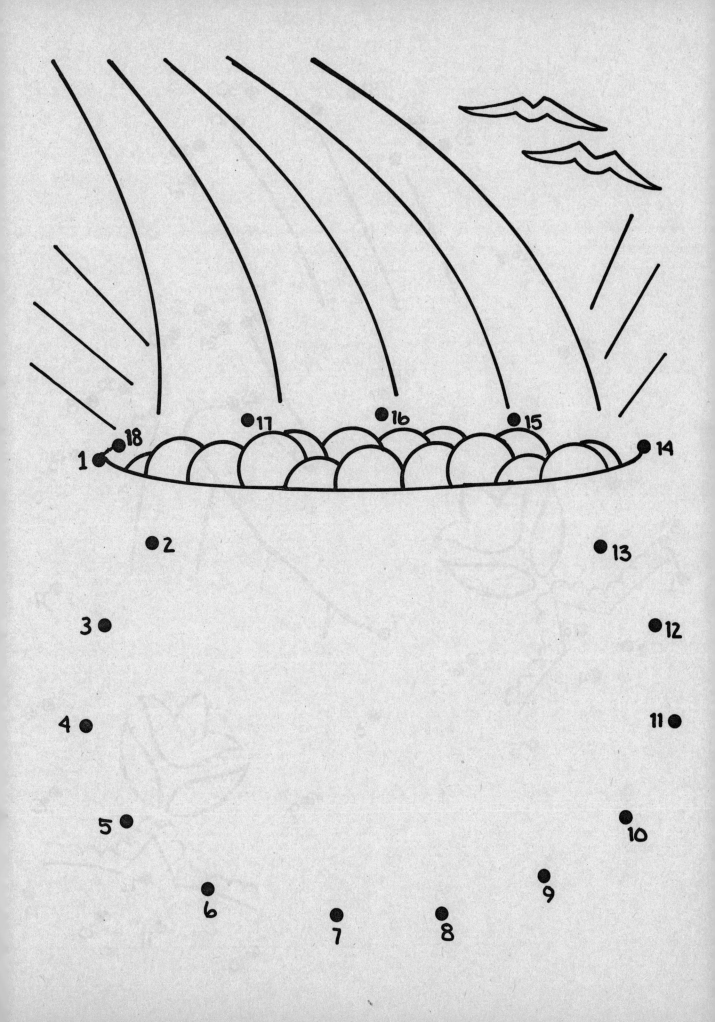

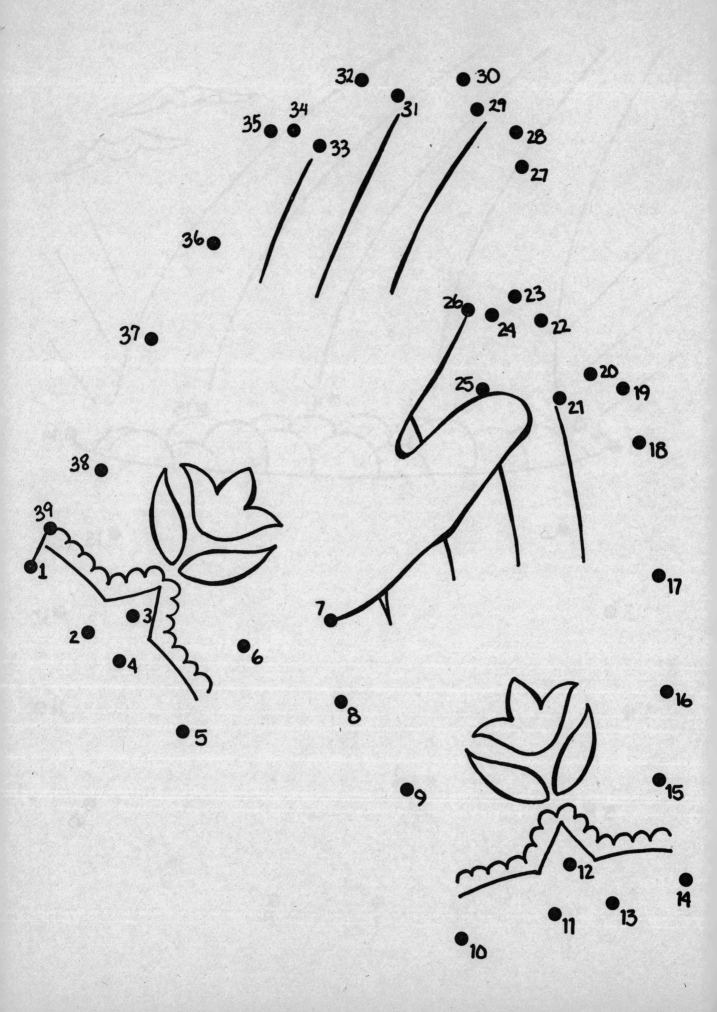

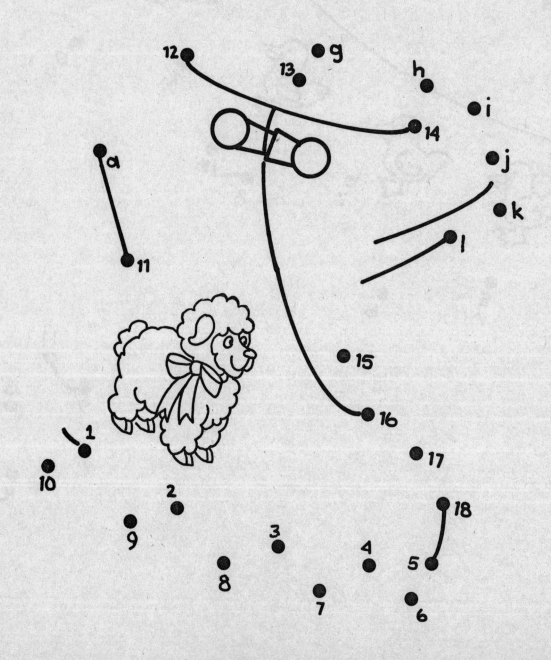

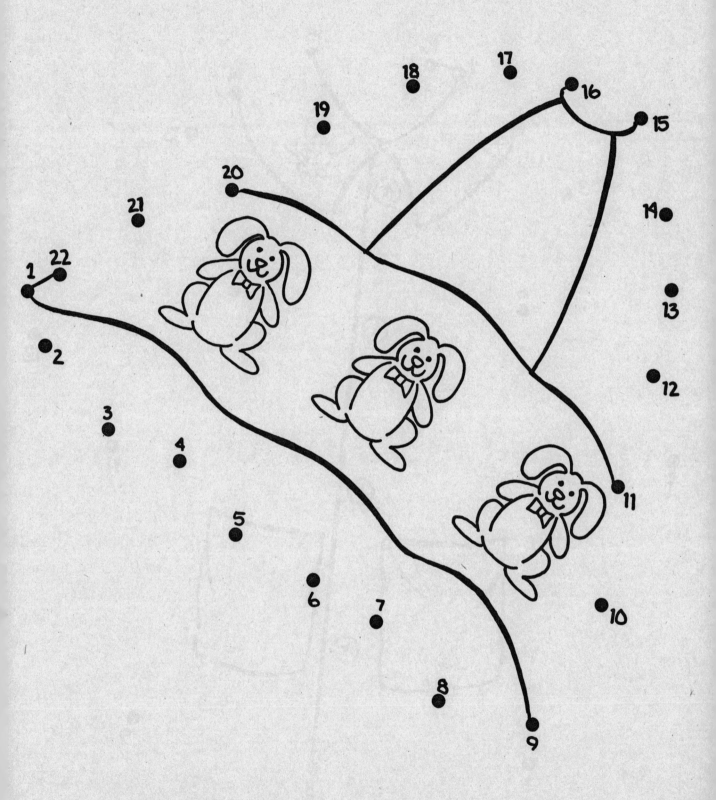

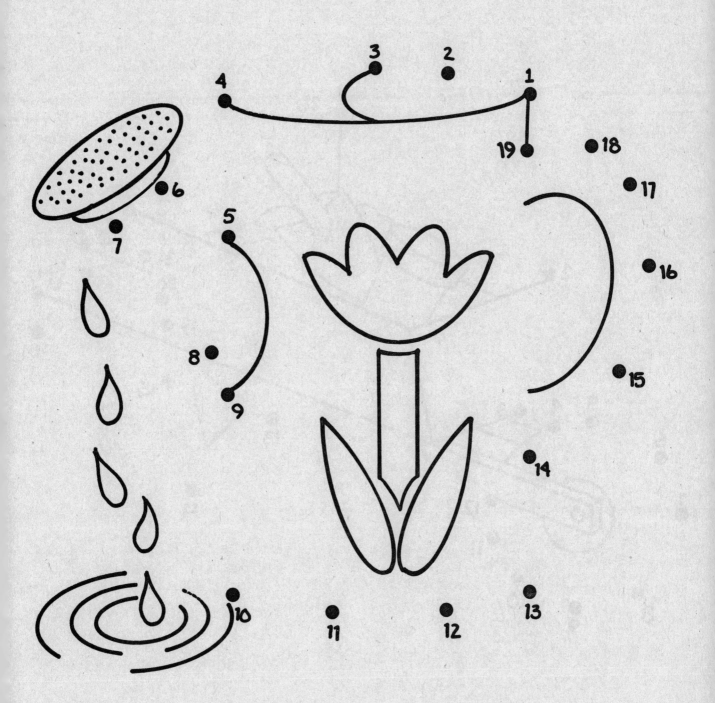

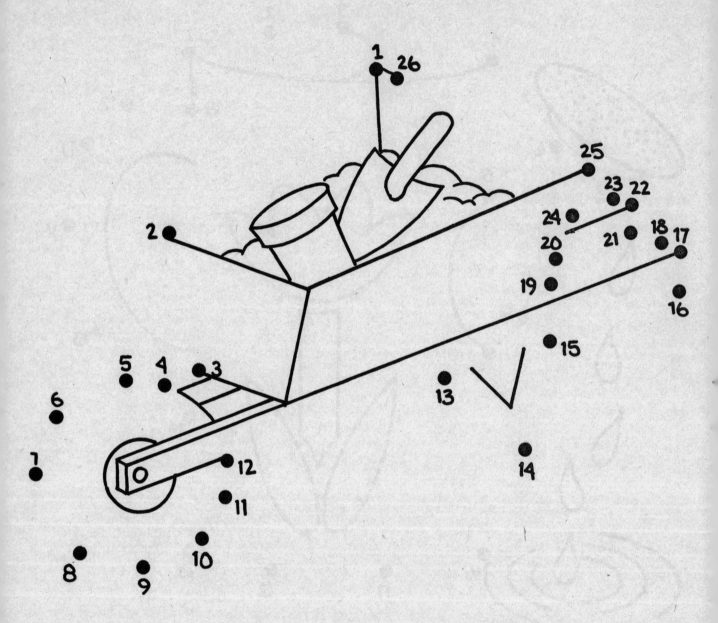

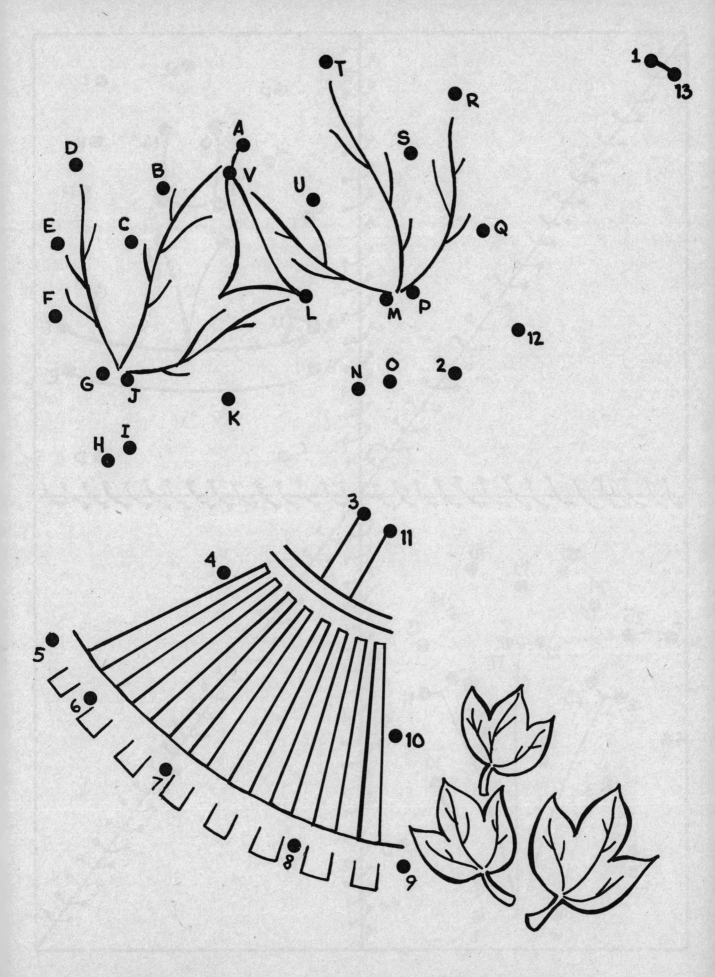

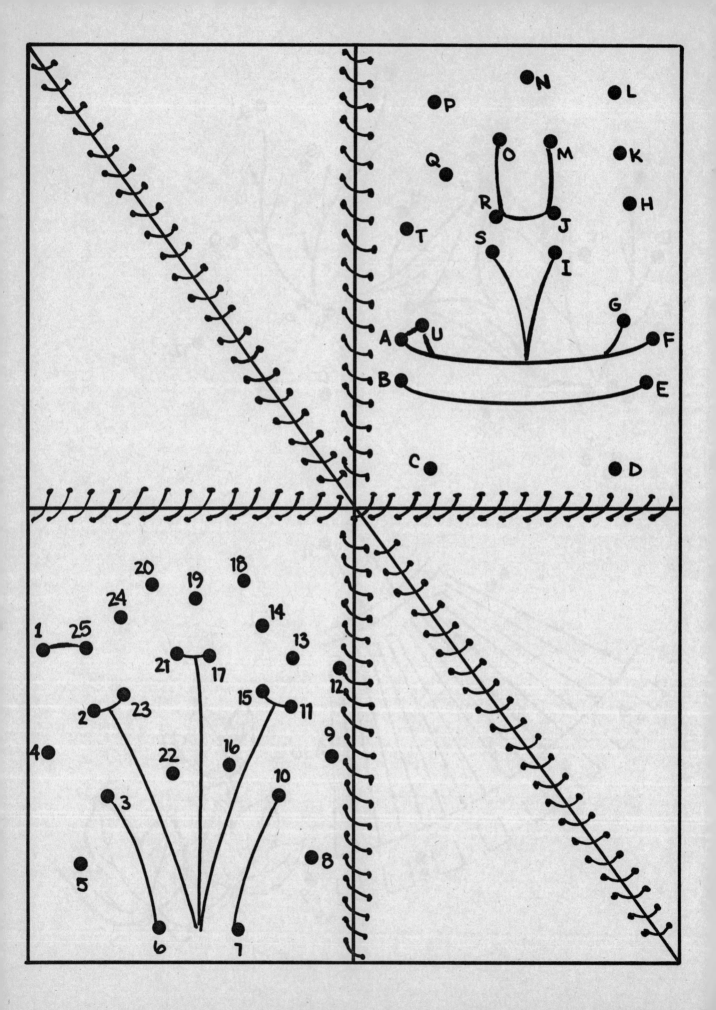

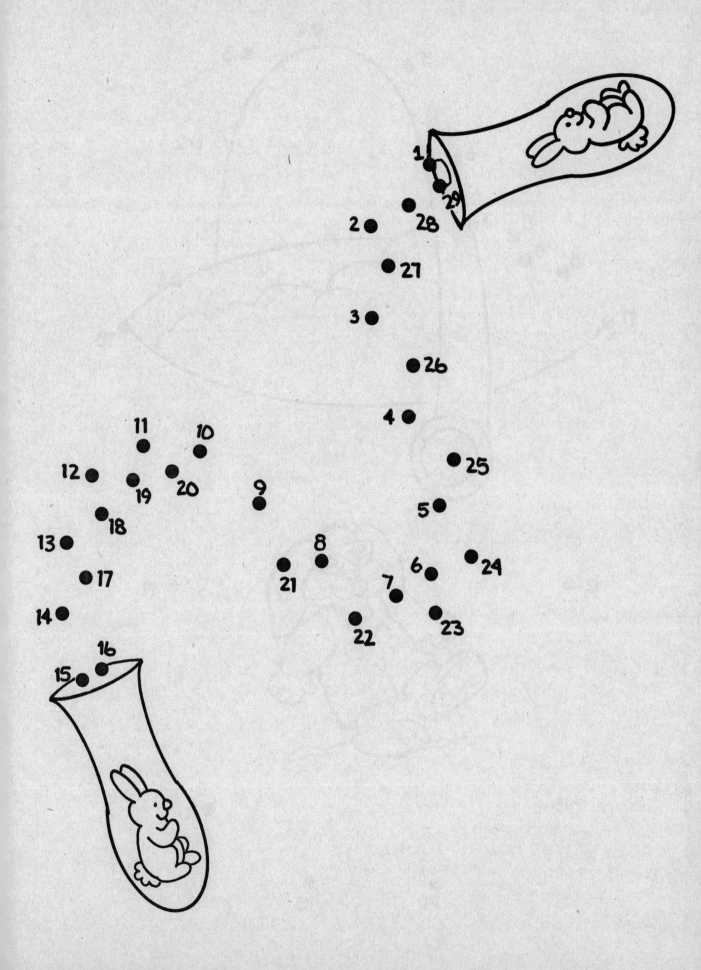

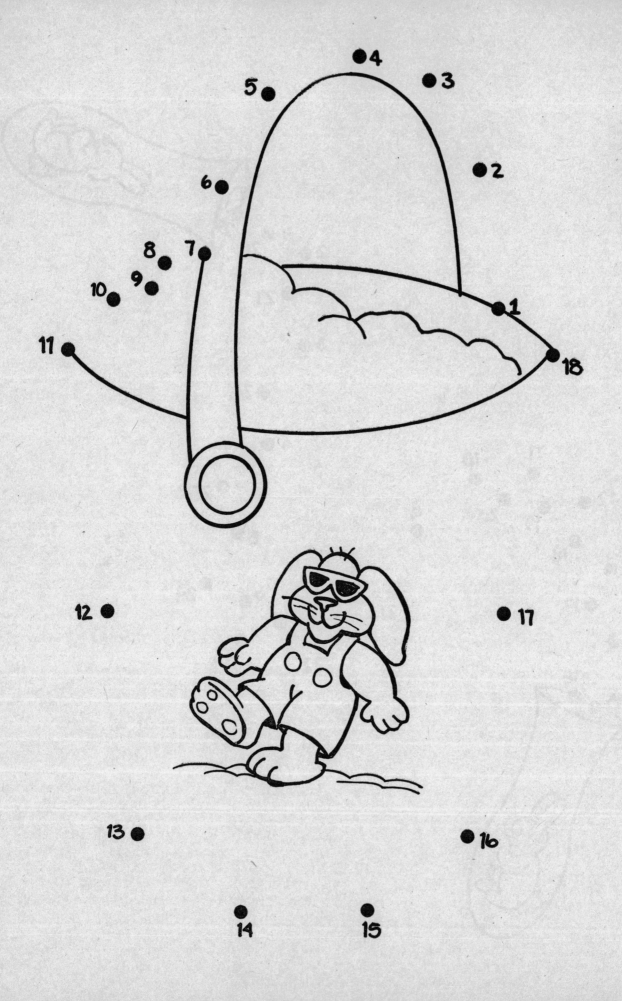

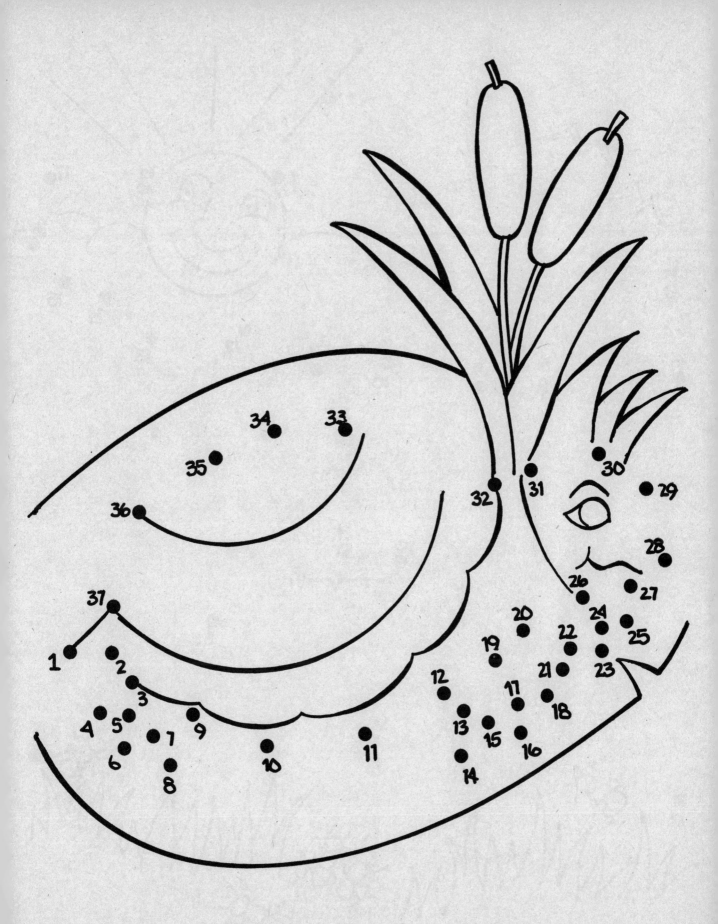

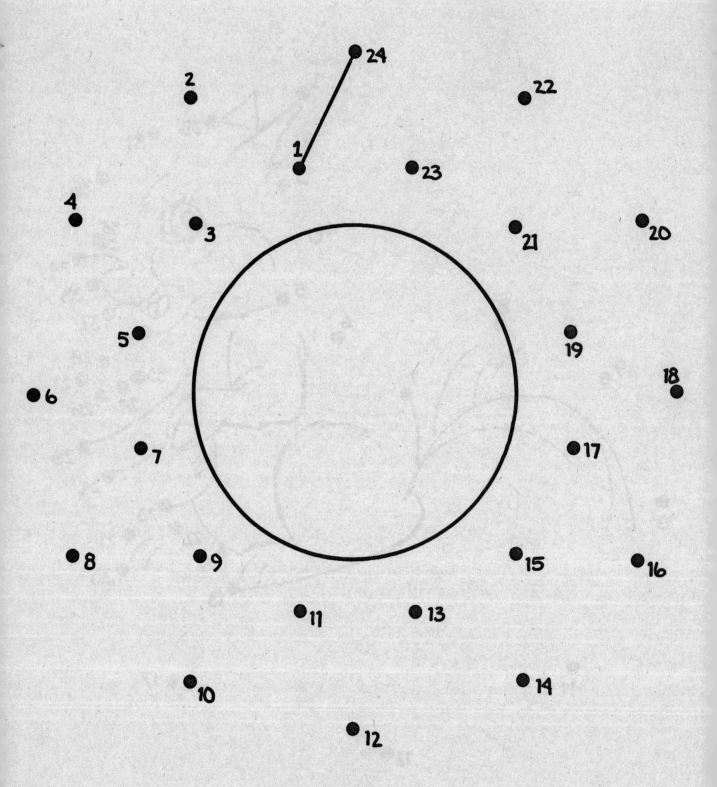

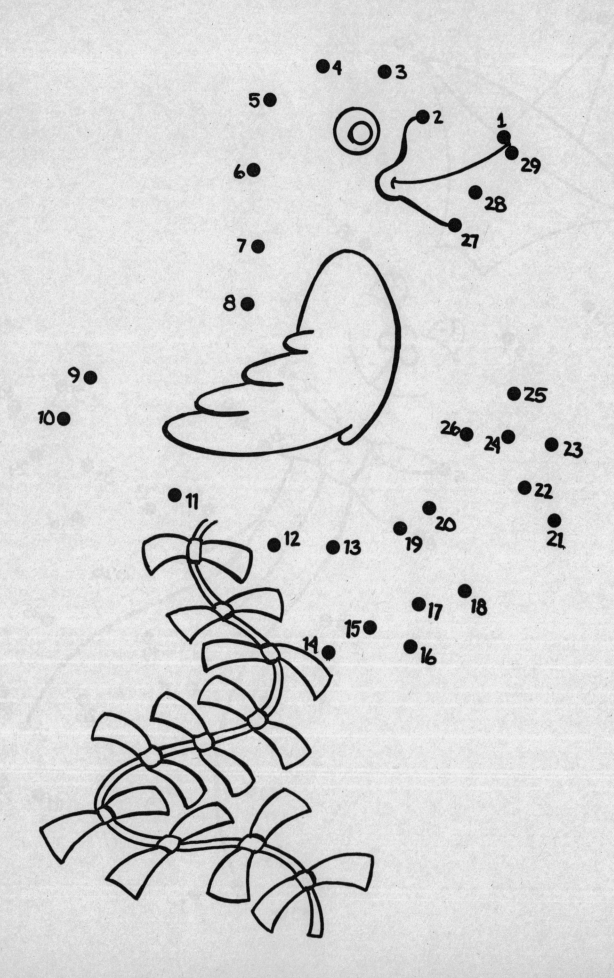

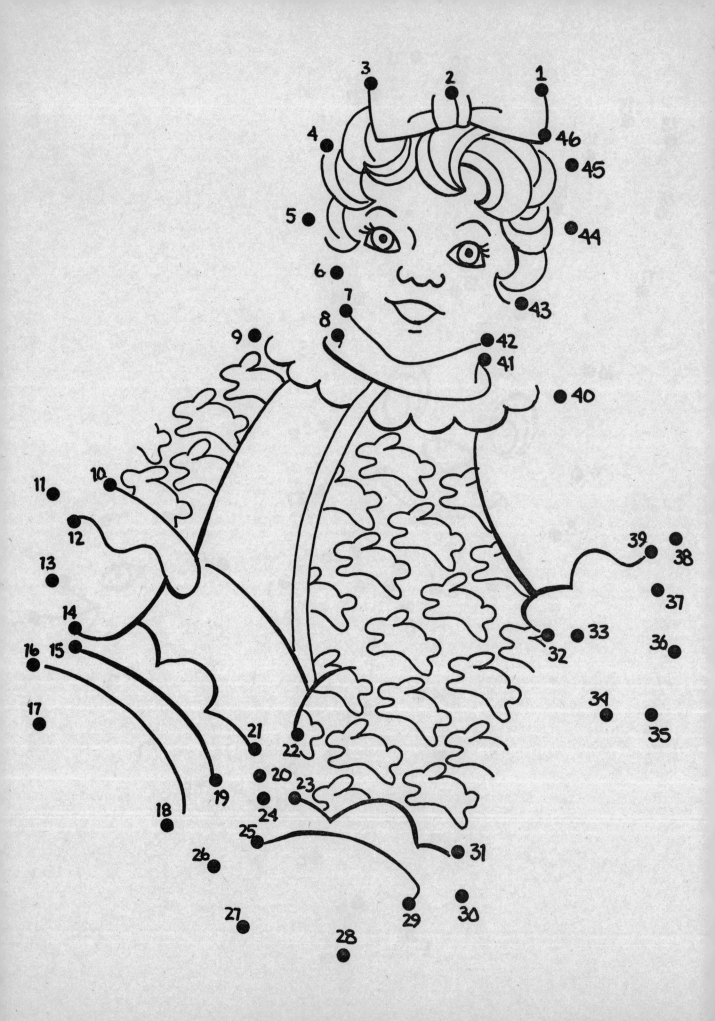

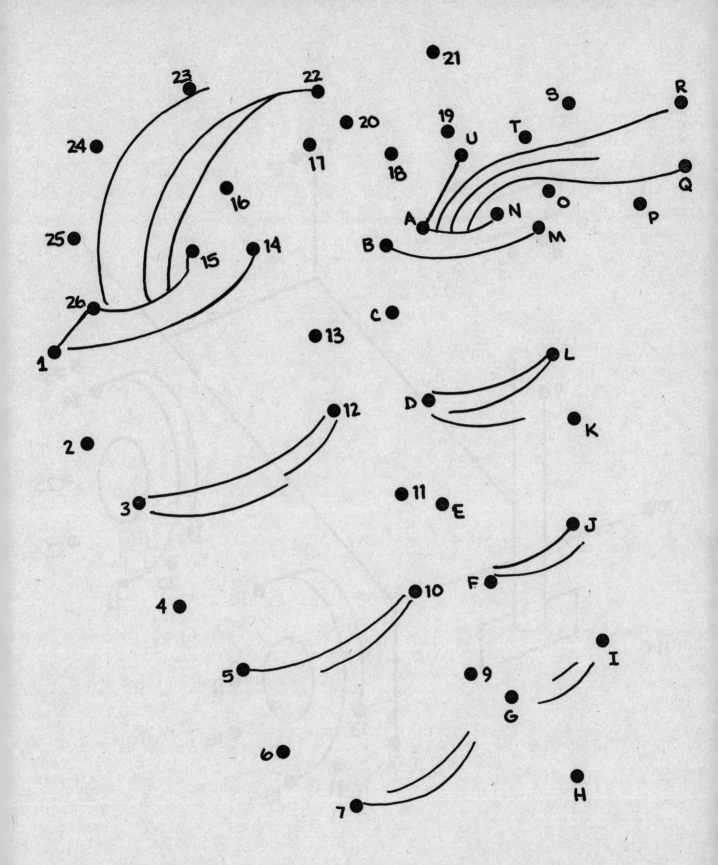

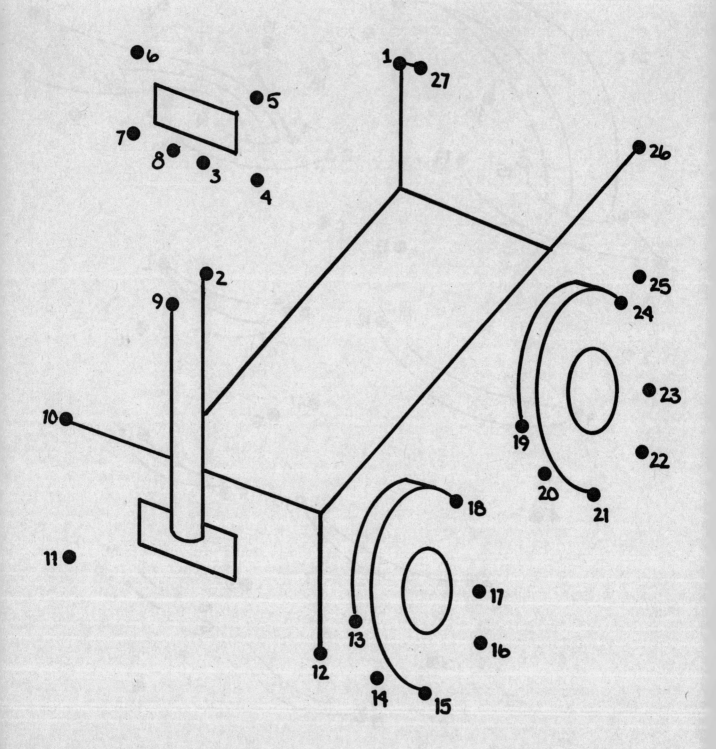

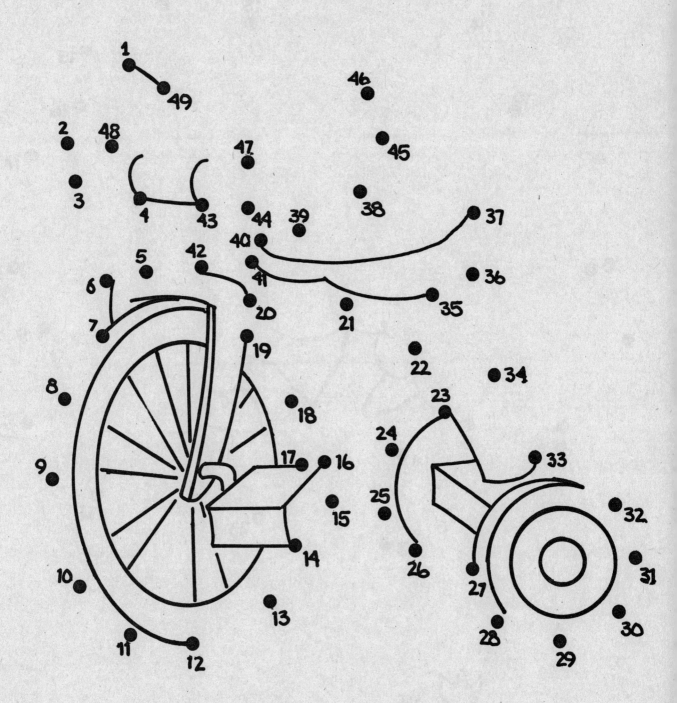

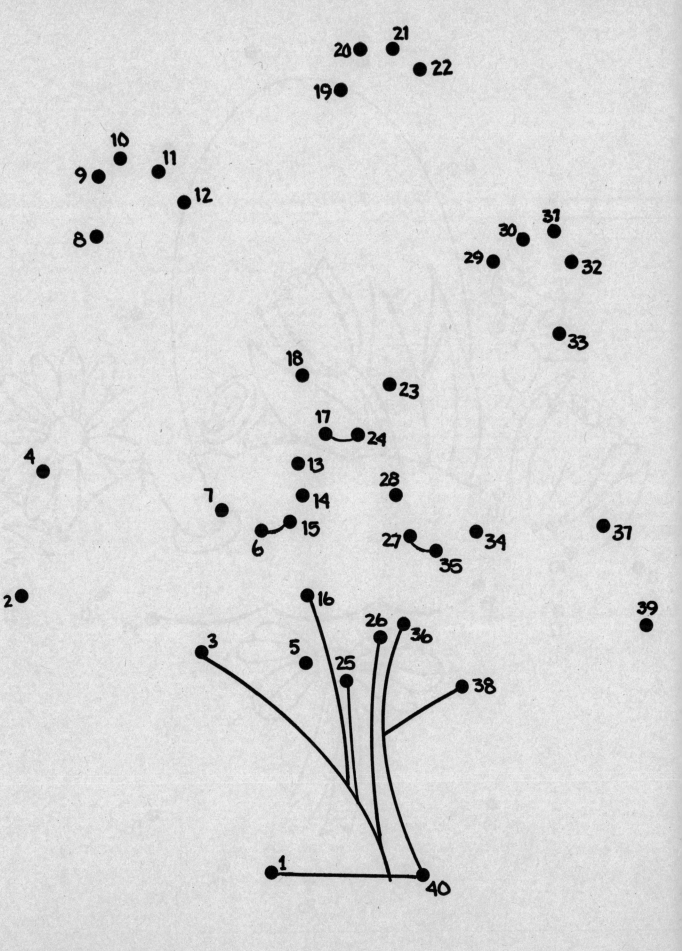